FOR MAXWELL EMERSON ENGLAND
"MAX"
THE NEW KID IN OUR FAMILY
—L.E.

TO MY FAMILY, CREATORS
AND NURTURERS OF DREAMS
—T. F.

Margaret K. McElderry Books
An imprint of Simon & Schuster Children's Publishing Division
1230 Avenue of the Americas
New York, New York 10020

Text copyright © 1998 by Linda England
Illustrations copyright © 1998 by Teresa Flavin
Book design by Angela Carlino
The text of this book is set in Egyptian 710
The illustrations were rendered in gouache on tinted paper
Printed in Hong Kong by South China Printing Co. (1988) Ltd.
First Edition
10 9 8 7 6 5 4 3 2 1
Library of Congress Cataloging-in-Publication Data:
England, Linda.
The old cotton blues / Linda England; illustrated by Teresa Flavin.—1st ed.
p. cm.
Summary: Dexter, who desperately wants to play a musical instrument,
learns to play the harmonica with the help of the old musician Johnny Cotton.
ISBN 0-689-81074-1
[1. Harmonica—Fiction. 2. Musicians—Fiction.] I. Flavin, Teresa, ill. II. Title.
PZ7.E71301   1998
[E]—dc20   96-28535   CIP   AC

THE
Old Cotton Blues

WRITTEN BY Linda England

ILLUSTRATED BY Teresa Flavin

MARGARET K. McELDERRY BOOKS

Dexter loved three things:

his mama, the smell of pork chops frying,

and the sound of Johnny Cotton's clarinet.

That clarinet could make Dexter feel

the blue-down blues, and the deep-down-shaking,

slow-laughing feel-goods.

Johnny Cotton was swaying and playing.

Dexter was stepping, slow stepping,

and dreaming a dream about playing,

and holding music in his hands

just like Johnny Cotton.

Johnny Cotton's song slipped into silence.

His voice was like some preacher's,

soft and kind of sunny.

"What's my boy dreaming of?

What words this old clarinet saying to you?"

"It's telling me to play," said Dexter.

"To blow the feelings from my soul.

Mama says I'm bursting with music."

Johnny Cotton said, "You got to smile at

your mama. Flash her that old razzle-dazzle.

Tell her you want to blow blues on your own clarinet."

Dexter asked, "Mama, oh Mama, please."

But Mama said, "Our money's for rent and the

pork chops you love. You know your wishes are

my wishes, Baby. I sure would if I could."

Dexter was feeling the

no-clarinet blues.

Feeling the sad place inside.

Feet scuffing the pavement,

scuffing a disappointed sound.

Johnny Cotton said, "That's a dream gone

for now. How about a new

dream of standing next to me playing a

Mississippi harp?

"We'll fix your blue-down blues.

We'll fix 'em with a story about

my daddy

and his Mississippi harp.

"My daddy's in heaven,

where the sky shines gold,

playing blues for angels,

making sunlight dance.

"Daddy played the harmonica,

a silver Mississippi harp.

Cupped it to his lips with great brown hands,

blew the sounds that made people weep and laugh.

And people called my daddy's music 'the Old Cotton Blues.'

"Hold out your hands.

Take this Mississippi harp, from my

daddy, to me, to you.

You got a soul bursting with music.

Practice, Dexter, and soon you'll play.

"Let your lips and your hands slide

along its old silver sides.

Blow your soul.

Play your feelings.

Cry the blues.

Laugh your joy.

You're holding music in your hands, little boy."

Dexter blew.

Those first sounds came hollering,

mingle-mangle, mishamasha music.

Dexter's mama said, "Keep trying, Baby."

Trying

Blowing

Thinking

Playing.

And then one day Dexter played.

He blew the pleasant, sweet sounds

that made him a music maker,

a player of his feelings.

Johnny Cotton was swaying and playing

his clarinet.

Dexter was swaying and playing

his silver harmonica.

Side by side they played the blue-down blues

and the deep-down-shaking, slow-laughing feel-goods.

Playing the Old Cotton Blues.

Dexter loved four things:

his mama, the smell of pork chops frying,

the sound of **Johnny Cotton's** clarinet,

and coaxing songs from his silver harmonica.